SHADOWS IN THE MOONLIGHT

SHADOWS IN THE MOONLIGHT

ROBERT E. HOWARD

CLASSY PUBLISHING

Shadows in the Moonlight
Published by Classy Publishing @ 2021

www.classypublishing.com

ISBN: 978-93-5522-009-7

Cover design & Layout by satyacoverdesign.com
contact@satyacoverdesign.com

1

A swift crashing of horses through the tall reeds; a heavy fall, a despairing cry. From the dying steed there staggered up its rider, a slender girl in sandals and girdled tunic. Her dark hair fell over her white shoulders, her eyes were those of a trapped animal. She did not look at the jungle of reeds that hemmed in the little clearing, nor at the blue waters that lapped the low shore behind her. Her wide-eyed gaze was fixed in agonized intensity on the horseman who pushed through the reedy screen and dismounted before her.

He was a tall man, slender, but hard as steel. From head to heel he was clad in light silvered mesh-mail that fitted his supple form like a glove. From under the dome-shaped, gold-chased helmet his brown eyes regarded her mockingly.

'Stand back!' her voice shrilled with terror. 'Touch me not, Shah Amurath, or I will throw myself into the water and drown!'

He laughed, and his laughter was like the purr of a sword sliding from a silken sheath.

'No, you will not drown, Olivia, daughter of confusion, for the marge is too shallow, and I can catch you before you can reach the deeps. You gave me a merry chase, by the gods, and all my men are far behind us. But there is no horse west of Vilayet that can distance Irem for long.' He nodded at the tall, slender-legged desert stallion behind him.

'Let me go!' begged the girl, tears of despair staining her face. 'Have I not suffered enough? Is there any humiliation, pain or degradation you have not heaped on me? How long must my torment last?'

'As long as I find pleasure in your whimperings, your pleas, tears and writhings,' he answered with a smile that would have seemed gentle to a stranger. 'You are strangely virile, Olivia. I wonder if I shall ever weary of you, as I have always wearied of women before. You are ever fresh and unsullied, in spite of me. Each new day with you brings a new delight.

'But come—let us return to Akif, where the people are still feting the conqueror of the miserable *kozaki*; while he, the conqueror, is engaged in recapturing a wretched fugitive, a foolish, lovely, idiotic runaway!'

'No!' She recoiled, turning toward the waters lapping bluely among the reeds.

'Yes!' His flash of open anger was like a spark struck from flint. With a quickness her tender limbs could not approximate, he caught her wrist, twisting it in pure wanton cruelty until she screamed and sank to her knees.

'Slut! I should drag you back to Akif at my horse's tail, but I will be merciful and carry you on my saddle-bow, for which favor you shall humbly thank me, while—'

He released her with a startled oath and sprang back, his saber flashing out, as a terrible apparition burst from the reedy jungle sounding an inarticulate cry of hate.

Olivia, staring up from the ground, saw what she took to be either a savage or a madman advancing on Shah Amurath in an attitude of deadly menace. He was powerfully built, naked but for a girdled loincloth, which was stained with blood and crusted with dried mire. His black mane was matted with mud and clotted blood; there were streaks of dried blood on his chest and limbs, dried blood on the long straight sword he gripped in his right hand. From under the tangle of his locks, bloodshot eyes glared like coals of blue fire.

'You Hyrkanian dog!' mouthed this apparition in a barbarous accent. 'The devils of vengeance have brought you here!'

'*Kozak!*' ejaculated Shah Amurath, recoiling. 'I did not know a dog of you escaped! I thought you all lay stiff on the steppe, by Ilbars River.'

'All but me, damn you!' cried the other. 'Oh, I've dreamed of such a meeting as this, while I crawled on my belly through the brambles, or lay under rocks while the ants gnawed my flesh, or crouched in the mire up to my mouth—I dreamed, but never hoped it would come to pass. Oh, gods of Hell, how I have yearned for this!'

The stranger's bloodthirsty joy was terrible to behold. His jaws champed spasmodically, froth appeared on his blackened lips.

'Keep back!' ordered Shah Amurath, watching him narrowly.

'Ha!' It was like the bark of a timber wolf. 'Shah Amurath, the great Lord of Akif! Oh, damn you, how I love the sight of you—you, who fed my comrades to the vultures, who tore them between wild horses, blinded and maimed and mutilated them—*ai*, you dog, you filthy dog!' His voice rose to a maddened scream, and he charged.

In spite of the terror of his wild appearance, Olivia looked to see him fall at the first crossing of the blades. Madman or savage, what could he do, naked, against the mailed chief of Akif?

There was an instant when the blades flamed and licked, seeming barely to touch each other and leap apart; then the broadsword flashed past the saber and descended terrifically on Shah Amurath's shoulder. Olivia cried out at the fury of that stroke. Above the crunch of the rending mail, she distinctly heard the snap of the shoulder-bone. The Hyrkanian reeled back, suddenly ashen, blood spurting over the links of his hauberk; his saber slipped from his nerveless fingers.

'Quarter!' he gasped.

'Quarter?' There was a quiver of frenzy in the stranger's voice. 'Quarter such as you gave us, you swine!'

Olivia closed her eyes. This was no longer battle, but butchery, frantic, bloody, impelled by an hysteria of fury and hate, in which culminated the sufferings of battle, massacre, torture, and fear-ridden, thirst-maddened, hunger-haunted flight. Though Olivia knew that Shah Amurath deserved no mercy or pity from any living creature, yet she closed her eyes and pressed her hands over her ears, to shut out the sight of that dripping sword that rose and fell with the sound of a butcher's cleaver, and the gurgling cries that dwindled away and ceased.

She opened her eyes, to see the stranger turning away from a gory travesty that only vaguely resembled a human being. The man's breast heaved with exhaustion or passion; his brow was beaded with sweat; his right hand was splashed with blood.

He did not speak to her, or even glance toward her. She saw him stride through the reeds that grew at the water's edge, stoop, and tug at something. A boat wallowed out of its hiding-place among the stalks. Then she divined his intention, and was galvanized into action.

'Oh, wait!' she wailed, staggering up and running toward him. 'Do not leave me! Take me with you!'

He wheeled and stared at her. There was a difference in his bearing. His bloodshot eyes were sane. It was as if the blood he had just shed had quenched the fire of his frenzy.

'Who are you?' he demanded.

'I am called Olivia. I was *his* captive. I ran away. He followed me. That's why he came here. Oh, do not leave me here! His warriors are not far behind him. They will find his corpse—they will find me near it—oh!' She moaned in her terror and wrung her white hands.

He stared at her in perplexity.

'Would you be better off with me?' he demanded. 'I am a barbarian, and I know from your looks that you fear me.'

'Yes, I fear you,' she replied, too distracted to dissemble. 'My flesh crawls at the horror of your aspect. But I fear the Hyrkanians more. Oh, let me go with you! They will put me to the torture if they find me beside their dead lord.'

'Come, then.' He drew aside, and she stepped quickly into the boat, shrinking from contact with him. She seated herself in the bow, and he stepped into the boat, pushed off with an oar, and using it as a paddle, worked his way tortuously among the tall stalks until they glided out into open water. Then he set to work with both oars, rowing with great, smooth, even strokes, the heavy muscles of arms and shoulders and back rippling in rhythm to his exertions.

There was silence for some time, the girl crouching in the bows, the man tugging at the oars. She watched him with timorous fascination. It was evident that he was not an Hyrkanian, and he did not resemble the Hyborian races. There was a wolfish hardness about him that marked the barbarian. His features, allowing for the strains and stains of battle and his hiding in the marshes, reflected that same untamed wildness, but they were neither evil nor degenerate.

'Who are you?' she asked. 'Shah Amurath called you a *kozak*; were you of that band?'

'I am Conan, of Cimmeria,' he grunted. 'I was with the *kozaki*, as the Hyrkanian dogs called us.'

She knew vaguely that the land he named lay far to the northwest, beyond the farthest boundaries of the different kingdoms of her race.

'I am a daughter of the King of Ophir,' she said. 'My father sold me to a Shemite chief, because I would not marry a prince of Koth.'

The Cimmerian grunted in surprize.

Her lips twisted in a bitter smile. 'Aye, civilized men sell their children as slaves to savages, sometimes. They call your race barbaric, Conan of Cimmeria.'

'We do not sell our children,' he growled, his chin jutting truculently.

'Well—I was sold. But the desert man did not misuse me. He wished to buy the good will of Shah Amurath, and I was among the gifts he brought to Akif of the purple gardens. Then—' She shuddered and hid her face in her hands.

'I should be lost to all shame,' she said presently. 'Yet each memory stings me like a slaver's whip. I abode in Shah Amurath's palace, until some weeks agone he rode out with his hosts to do battle with a band of invaders who were ravaging the borders of Turan. Yesterday he returned in triumph, and a great fete was made to honor him. In the drunkenness and rejoicing, I found an opportunity to steal out of the city on a stolen horse.

I had thought to escape—but he followed, and about midday came up with me. I outran his vassals, but him I could not escape. Then you came.'

'I was lying hid in the reeds,' grunted the barbarian. 'I was one of those dissolute rogues, the Free Companions, who burned and looted along the borders. There were five thousand of us, from a score of races and tribes. We had been serving as mercenaries for a rebel prince in eastern Koth, most of us, and when he made peace with his cursed sovereign, we were out of employment; so we took to plundering the outlying dominions of Koth, Zamora and Turan impartially. A week ago Shah Amurath trapped us near the banks of Ilbars with fifteen thousand men. Mitra! The skies were black with vultures. When the lines broke, after a whole day of fighting, some tried to break through to the north, some to the west. I doubt if any escaped. The steppes were covered with horsemen riding down the fugitives. I broke for the east, and finally reached the edge of the marshes that border this part of Vilayet.

'I've been hiding in the morasses ever since. Only the day before yesterday the riders ceased beating up the reed-brakes, searching for just such fugitives as I. I've squirmed and burrowed and hidden like a snake, feasting on musk-rats I caught and ate raw, for lack of fire to cook them. This dawn I found this boat hidden among the reeds. I hadn't intended going out on the sea until night, but after I killed Shah Amurath, I knew his mailed dogs would be close at hand.'

'And what now?'

'We shall doubtless be pursued. If they fail to see the marks left by the boat, which I covered as well as I could, they'll guess anyway that we took to sea, after they fail to find us among the marshes. But we have a start, and I'm going to haul at these oars until we reach a safe place.'

'Where shall we find that?' she asked hopelessly. 'Vilayet is an Hyrkanian pond.'

'Some folk don't think so,' grinned Conan grimly; 'notably the slaves that have escaped from galleys and become pirates.'

'But what are your plans?'

'The southwestern shore is held by the Hyrkanians for hundreds of miles. We still have a long way to go before we pass beyond their northern boundaries. I intend to go northward until I think we have passed them. Then we'll turn westward, and try to land on the shore bordered by the uninhabited steppes.'

'Suppose we meet pirates, or a storm?' she asked. 'And we shall starve on the steppes.'

'Well,' he reminded her, 'I didn't ask you to come with me.'

'I am sorry.' She bowed her shapely dark head. 'Pirates, storms, starvation—they are all kinder than the people of Turan.'

'Aye.' His dark face grew somber. 'I haven't done with them yet. Be at ease, girl. Storms are rare on Vilayet at this time of year. If we make the steppes, we shall not starve. I was reared in a naked land. It was those cursed marshes, with their stench and stinging flies, that nigh unmanned me. I am at home in the high lands. As for pirates—' He grinned enigmatically, and bent to the oars.

The sun sank like a dull-glowing copper ball into a lake of fire. The blue of the sea merged with the blue of the sky, and both turned to soft dark velvet, clustered with stars and the mirrors of stars. Olivia reclined in the bows of the gently rocking boat, in a state dreamy and unreal. She experienced an illusion that she was floating in midair, stars beneath her as well as above. Her silent companion was etched vaguely against the softer darkness. There was no break or falter in the rhythm of his oars; he might have been a fantasmal oarsman, rowing her across the dark lake of Death. But the edge of her fear was dulled, and, lulled by the monotony of motion, she passed into a quiet slumber.

Dawn was in her eyes when she awakened, aware of a ravenous hunger. It was a change in the motion of the boat that had roused her; Conan was resting on his oars, gazing beyond her. She realized that he had rowed all night without pause, and marvelled at his iron endurance. She twisted about to follow his stare, and saw a green wall of trees and shrubbery rising from the water's edge and sweeping away in a wide curve, enclosing a small bay whose waters lay still as blue glass.

'This is one of the many islands that dot this inland sea,' said Conan. 'They are supposed to be uninhabited. I've heard the Hyrkanians seldom visit them. Besides, they generally hug the shores in their galleys, and we have come a long way. Before sunset we were out of sight of the mainland.'

With a few strokes he brought the boat in to shore and made the painter fast to the arching root of a tree which rose from the water's edge. Stepping ashore, he reached out a hand to help Olivia. She took it, wincing slightly at the bloodstains upon it, feeling a hint of the dynamic strength that lurked in the barbarian's thews.

A dreamy quiet lay over the woods that bordered the blue bay. Then somewhere, far back among the trees, a bird lifted its morning song. A breeze whispered through the leaves, and set them to murmuring. Olivia found herself listening intently for something, she knew not what. What might be lurking amid those nameless woodlands?

As she peered timidly into the shadows between the trees, something swept into the sunlight with a swift whirl of wings: a great parrot which dropped on to a leafy branch and swayed there, a gleaming image of jade and crimson. It turned its crested head sidewise and regarded the invaders with glittering eyes of jet.

'Crom!' muttered the Cimmerian. 'Here is the grandfather of all parrots. He must be a thousand years old! Look at the evil wisdom of his eyes. What mysteries do you guard, Wise Devil?'

Abruptly the bird spread its flaming wings and, soaring from its perch, cried out harshly: '*Yagkoolan yok tha, xuthalla!*' and with a wild screech of horribly human laughter, rushed away through the trees to vanish in the opalescent shadows.

Olivia stared after it, feeling the cold hand of nameless foreboding touch her supple spine.

'What did it say?' she whispered.

'Human words, I'll swear,' answered Conan; 'but in what tongue I can't say.'

'Nor I,' returned the girl. 'Yet it must have learned them from human lips. Human, or—' she gazed into the leafy fastness and shuddered slightly, without knowing why.

'Crom, I'm hungry!' grunted the Cimmerian. 'I could eat a whole buffalo. We'll look for fruit; but first I'm going to cleanse myself of this dried mud and blood. Hiding in marshes is foul business.'

So saying, he laid aside his sword, and wading out shoulder-deep into the blue water, went about his ablutions. When he emerged, his clean-cut bronze limbs shone, his streaming black mane was no longer matted. His blue eyes, though they smoldered with unquenchable fire, were no longer murky or bloodshot. But the tigerish suppleness of limb and the dangerous aspect of feature were not altered.

Strapping on his sword once more, he motioned the girl to follow him, and they left the shore, passing under the leafy arches of the great branches. Underfoot lay a short green sward which cushioned their tread. Between the trunks of the trees they caught glimpses of faery-like vistas.

Presently Conan grunted in pleasure at the sight of golden and russet globes hanging in clusters among the leaves. Indicating that the girl should seat herself on a fallen tree, he filled her lap with the exotic delicacies, and then himself fell to with unconcealed gusto.

'Ishtar!' said he, between mouthfuls. 'Since Ilbars I have lived on rats, and roots I dug out of the stinking mud. This is sweet to the palate, though not very filling. Still, it will serve if we eat enough.'

Olivia was too busy to reply. The sharp edge of the Cimmerian's hunger blunted, he began to gaze at his fair companion with more interest than previously, noting the lustrous clusters of her dark hair, the peach-bloom tints of her dainty skin, and the rounded contours of her lithe figure which the scanty silk tunic displayed to full advantage.

Finishing her meal, the object of his scrutiny looked up, and meeting his burning, slit-eyed gaze, she changed color and the remnants of the fruit slipped from her fingers.

Without comment, he indicated with a gesture that they should continue their explorations, and rising, she followed him out of the trees and into a glade, the farther end of which was bounded by a dense thicket. As they stepped into the open there was a ripping crash in this thicket, and Conan, bounding aside and carrying the girl with him, narrowly saved them from something that rushed through the air and struck a tree-trunk with a thunderous impact.

Whipping out his sword, Conan bounded across the glade and plunged into the thicket. Silence ensued, while Olivia crouched on the sward, terrified and bewildered. Presently Conan emerged, a puzzled scowl on his face.

'Nothing in that thicket,' he growled. 'But there was something—'

He studied the missile that had so narrowly missed them, and grunted incredulously, as if unable to credit his own senses. It was a huge block of greenish stone which lay on the sward at the foot of the tree, whose wood its impact had splintered.

'A strange stone to find on an uninhabited island,' growled Conan.

Olivia's lovely eyes dilated in wonder. The stone was a symmetrical block, indisputably cut and shaped by human hands. And it was astonishingly massive. The Cimmerian grasped it with both hands, and with legs braced and the muscles standing out on his arms and back in straining knots, he heaved it above his head and cast it from him, exerting every ounce of nerve and sinew. It fell a few feet in front of him. Conan swore.

'No man living could throw that rock across this glade. It's a task for siege engines. Yet here there are no mangonels or ballistas.'

'Perhaps it was thrown by some such engine from afar,' she suggested.

He shook his head. 'It didn't fall from above. It came from yonder thicket. See how the twigs are broken? It was thrown as a man might throw a pebble. But who? What? Come!'

She hesitantly followed him into the thicket. Inside the outer ring of leafy brush, the undergrowth was less dense. Utter silence brooded over all. The springy sward gave no sign of footprint. Yet from this mysterious thicket had hurtled that boulder, swift and deadly. Conan bent closer to the sward, where the grass was crushed down here and there. He shook his head angrily. Even to his keen eyes it gave no clue as to what had stood or trodden there. His gaze roved to the green roof above their heads, a solid ceiling of thick leaves and interwoven arches. And he froze suddenly.

Then rising, sword in hand, he began to back away, thrusting Olivia behind him.

'Out of here, quick!' he urged in a whisper that congealed the girl's blood.

'What is it? What do you see?'

'Nothing,' he answered guardedly, not halting his wary retreat.

'But what is it, then? What lurks in this thicket?'

'Death!' he answered, his gaze still fixed on the brooding jade arches that shut out the sky.

Once out of the thicket, he took her hand and led her swiftly through the thinning trees, until they mounted a grassy slope, sparsely treed, and emerged upon a low plateau, where the grass grew taller and the trees were few and scattered. And in the midst of that plateau rose a long broad structure of crumbling greenish stone.

They gazed in wonder. No legends named such a building on any island of Vilayet. They approached it warily, seeing that moss and lichen crawled over the stones, and the broken roof gaped to the sky. On all sides lay bits and shards of masonry, half hidden in the waving grass, giving the impression that once many buildings rose there, perhaps a whole town. But now only the long hall-like structure rose against the sky, and its walls leaned drunkenly among the crawling vines.

Whatever doors had once guarded its portals had long rotted away. Conan and his companion stood in the broad entrance and stared inside. Sunlight streamed in through gaps in the walls and roof, making the interior a dim weave of light and shadow. Grasping his sword firmly, Conan entered, with the slouching gait of a hunting panther, sunken head and noiseless feet. Olivia tiptoed after him.

Once within, Conan grunted in surprize, and Olivia stifled a scream.

'Look! Oh, look!'

'I see,' he answered. 'Nothing to fear. They are statues.'

'But how life-like—and how evil!' she whispered, drawing close to him.

They stood in a great hall, whose floor was of polished stone, littered with dust and broken stones, which had fallen from the ceiling. Vines, growing between the stones, masked the apertures. The lofty roof, flat and undomed, was upheld by thick columns, marching in rows down the sides of the walls. And in each space between these columns stood a strange figure.

They were statues, apparently of iron, black and shining as if continually polished. They were life-sized, depicting tall, lithely powerful men, with cruel hawk-like faces. They were naked, and every swell, depression and contour of joint and sinew was represented with incredible realism. But the most life-like feature was their proud, intolerant faces. These features were not cast in the same mold. Each face possessed its own individual characteristics, though there was a tribal likeness between them all. There was none of the monotonous uniformity of decorative art, in the faces at least.

'They seem to be listening—and waiting!' whispered the girl uneasily.

Conan rang his hilt against one of the images.

'Iron,' he pronounced. 'But Crom! In what molds were they cast?'

He shook his head and shrugged his massive shoulders in puzzlement.

Olivia glanced timidly about the great silent hall. Only the ivy-grown stones, the tendril-clasped pillars, with the dark figures brooding between them, met her gaze. She shifted uneasily and wished to be gone, but the images held a strange fascination for her companion. He examined them in detail, and barbarian-like, tried to break off their limbs. But their material resisted his best efforts. He could neither disfigure nor dislodge from its niche a single image. At last he desisted, swearing in his wonder.

'What manner of men were these copied from?' he inquired of the world at large. 'These figures are black, yet they are not like negroes. I have never seen their like.'

'Let us go into the sunlight,' urged Olivia, and he nodded, with a baffled glance at the brooding shapes along the walls.

So they passed out of the dusky hall into the clear blaze of the summer sun. She was surprized to note its position in the sky; they had spent more time in the ruins than she had guessed.

'Let us take to the boat again,' she suggested. 'I am afraid here. It is a strange evil place. We do not know when we may be attacked by whatever cast the rock.'

'I think we're safe as long as we're not under the trees,' he answered. 'Come.'

The plateau, whose sides fell away toward the wooded shores on the east, west and south, sloped upward toward the north to abut on a tangle of rocky cliffs, the highest point of the island. Thither Conan took his way, suiting his long stride to his companion's gait. From time to time his glance rested inscrutably upon her, and she was aware of it.

They reached the northern extremity of the plateau, and stood gazing up the steep pitch of the cliffs. Trees grew thickly along the rim of the plateau east and west of the cliffs, and clung to the precipitous incline. Conan glanced at these trees suspiciously, but he began the ascent, helping his companion on the climb. The slope was not sheer, and was broken by ledges and boulders. The Cimmerian, born in a hill country, could have run up it like a cat, but Olivia found the going difficult. Again and again she felt herself lifted lightly off her feet and over some obstacle that would have taxed her strength to surmount, and her wonder grew at the sheer physical power of the man. She no longer found his touch repugnant. There was a promise of protection in his iron clasp.

At last they stood on the ultimate pinnacle, their hair stirring in the sea wind. From their feet the cliffs fell away sheerly three or four hundred feet to a narrow tangle of woodlands bordering the beach. Looking southward they saw the whole island lying like a great oval mirror, its bevelled edges sloping down swiftly into a rim of green, except where it broke in the pitch of the cliffs. As far as they could see, on all sides stretched the blue waters, still, placid, fading into dreamy hazes of distance.

'The sea is still,' sighed Olivia. 'Why should we not take up our journey again?'

Conan, poised like a bronze statue on the cliffs, pointed northward. Straining her eyes, Olivia saw a white fleck that seemed to hang suspended in the aching haze.

'What is it?'

'A sail.'

'Hyrkanians?'

'Who can tell, at this distance?'

'They will anchor here—search the island for us!' she cried in quick panic.

'I doubt it. They come from the north, so they can not be searching for us. They may stop for some other reason, in which case we'll have to hide as best we can. But I believe it's either pirate, or an Hyrkanian galley returning from some northern raid. In the latter case they are not likely to anchor here. But we can't put to sea until they've gone out of sight, for they're coming from the direction in which we must go. Doubtless they'll pass the island tonight, and at dawn we can go on our way.'

'Then we must spend the night here?' she shivered.

'It's safest.'

'Then let us sleep here, on the crags,' she urged.

He shook his head, glancing at the stunted trees, at the marching woods below, a green mass which seemed to send out tendrils straggling up the sides of the cliffs.

'Here are too many trees. We'll sleep in the ruins.'

She cried out in protest.

'Nothing will harm you there,' he soothed. 'Whatever threw the stone at us did not follow us out of the woods. There was nothing to show that any wild thing lairs in the ruins. Besides, you are soft-skinned, and used to shelter and dainties. I could sleep naked in the snow and feel no discomfort, but the dew would give you cramps, were we to sleep in the open.'

Olivia helplessly acquiesced, and they descended the cliffs, crossed the plateau and once more approached the gloomy, age-haunted ruins. By this time the sun was sinking below the plateau rim. They had found fruit in the trees near the cliffs, and these formed their supper, both food and drink.

The southern night swept down quickly, littering the dark blue sky with great white stars, and Conan entered the shadowy ruins, drawing the reluctant Olivia after him. She shivered at the sight of those tense black shadows in their niches along the walls. In the darkness that the starlight only faintly touched, she could not make out their outlines; she could only sense their attitude of waiting—waiting as they had waited for untold centuries.

Conan had brought a great armful of tender branches, well leafed. These he heaped to make a couch for her, and she lay upon it, with a curious sensation as of one lying down to sleep in a serpent's lair.

Whatever her forebodings, Conan did not share them. The Cimmerian sat down near her, his back against a pillar, his sword across his knees. His eyes gleamed like a panther's in the dusk.

'Sleep, girl,' said he. 'My slumber is light as a wolf's. Nothing can enter this hall without awaking me.'

Olivia did not reply. From her bed of leaves she watched the immobile figure, indistinct in the soft darkness. How strange, to move in fellowship with a barbarian, to be cared for and protected by one of a race, tales of which had frightened her as a child! He came of a people bloody, grim and ferocious. His kinship to the wild was apparent in his every action; it burned in his smoldering eyes. Yet he had not harmed her, and her worst oppressor had been a man the world called civilized. As a delicious languor stole over her relaxing limbs and she sank into foamy billows of slumber, her last waking thought was a drowsy recollection of the firm touch of Conan's fingers on her soft flesh.

2

Olivia dreamed, and through her dreams crawled a suggestion of lurking evil, like a black serpent writhing through flower gardens. Her dreams were fragmentary and colorful, exotic shards of a broken, unknown pattern, until they crystalized into a scene of horror and madness, etched against a background of cyclopean stones and pillars.

She saw a great hall, whose lofty ceiling was upheld by stone columns marching in even rows along the massive walls. Among these pillars fluttered great green and scarlet parrots, and the hall was thronged with black-skinned, hawk-faced warriors. They were not negroes. Neither they nor their garments nor weapons resembled anything of the world the dreamer knew.

They were pressing about one bound to a pillar: a slender white-skinned youth, with a cluster of golden curls about his alabaster brow. His beauty was not altogether human—like the dream of a god, chiseled out of living marble.

The black warriors laughed at him, jeered and taunted in a strange tongue. The lithe naked form writhed beneath their cruel hands. Blood trickled down the ivory thighs to spatter on the polished floor. The screams of the victim echoed through the hall; then lifting his head toward the ceiling and the skies beyond, he cried out a name in an awful voice. A dagger in an ebon hand cut short his cry, and the golden head rolled on the ivory breast.

As if in answer to that desperate cry, there was a rolling thunder as of celestial chariot-wheels, and a figure stood before the slayers, as if materialized out of empty air. The form was of a man, but no mortal man ever wore such an aspect of inhuman beauty. There was an unmistakable resemblance between him and the youth who dropped lifeless in his chains, but the alloy of humanity that softened the godliness of the youth was lacking in the features of the stranger, awful and immobile in their beauty.

The blacks shrank back before him, their eyes slits of fire. Lifting a hand, he spoke, and his tones echoed through the silent halls in deep rich waves of sound. Like men in a trance the black warriors fell back until they were ranged along the walls in regular lines. Then from the stranger's chiseled lips rang a terrible invocation and command: '*Yagkoolan yok tha, xuthalla!*'

At the blast of that awful cry, the black figures stiffened and froze. Over their limbs crept a curious rigidity, an unnatural petrification. The stranger touched the limp body of the youth, and the chains fell away from it. He lifted the corpse in his arms; then ere he turned away, his tranquil gaze swept again over the silent rows of ebony figures, and he pointed to the moon, which gleamed in through the casements. And they understood, those tense, waiting statues that had been men....

Olivia awoke, starting up on her couch of branches, a cold sweat beading her skin. Her heart pounded loud in the silence. She glanced wildly about. Conan slept against his pillar, his head fallen upon his massive breast. The silvery radiance of the late moon crept through the gaping roof, throwing long white lines along the dusty floor. She could see the images dimly, black, tense—waiting. Fighting down a rising hysteria, she saw the moonbeams rest lightly on the pillars and the shapes between.

What was that? A tremor among the shadows where the moonlight fell. A paralysis of horror gripped her, for where there should have been the immobility of death, there was movement: a slow twitching, a flexing and writhing of ebon limbs—an awful scream burst from her lips as she broke the bonds that held her mute and motionless. At her shriek Conan shot erect, teeth gleaming, sword lifted.

'The statues! The statues!—*Oh my God, the statues are coming to life!*'

And with the cry she sprang through a crevice in the wall, burst madly through the hindering vines, and ran, ran, ran—blind, screaming, witless—until a grasp on her arm brought her up short and she shrieked and fought against the arms that caught her, until a familiar voice penetrated the mists of her terror, and she saw Conan's face, a mask of bewilderment in the moonlight.

'What in Crom's name, girl? Did you have a nightmare?' His voice sounded strange and far away. With a sobbing gasp she threw her arms about his thick neck and clung to him convulsively, crying in panting catches.

'Where are they? Did they follow us?'

'Nobody followed us,' he answered.

She sat up, still clinging to him, and looked fearfully about. Her blind flight had carried her to the southern edge of the plateau. Just below them was the slope, its foot masked in the thick shadows of the woods. Behind them she saw the ruins looming in the high-swinging moon.

'Did you not see them?—The statues, moving, lifting their hands, their eyes glaring in the shadows?'

'I saw nothing,' answered the barbarian uneasily. 'I slept more soundly than usual, because it has been so long since I have slumbered the night through; yet I don't think anything could have entered the hall without waking me.'

'Nothing entered,' a laugh of hysteria escaped her. 'It was something there already. Ah, Mitra, we lay down to sleep among them, like sheep making their bed in the shambles!'

'What are you talking about?' he demanded. 'I woke at your cry, but before I had time to look about me, I saw you rush out through the crack in the wall. I pursued you, lest you come to harm. I thought you had a nightmare.'

'So I did!' she shivered. 'But the reality was more grisly than the dream. Listen!' And she narrated all that she had dreamed and thought to see.

Conan listened attentively. The natural skepticism of the sophisticated man was not his. His mythology contained ghouls, goblins, and necromancers. After she had finished, he sat silent, absently toying with his sword.

'The youth they tortured was like the tall man who came?' he asked at last.

'As like as son to father,' she answered, and hesitantly: 'If the mind could conceive of the offspring of a union of divinity with humanity, it would picture that youth. The gods of old times mated sometimes with mortal women, our legends tell us.'

'What gods?' he muttered.

'The nameless, forgotten ones. Who knows? They have gone back into the still waters of the lakes, the quiet hearts of the hills, the gulfs beyond the stars. Gods are no more stable than men.'

'But if these shapes were men, blasted into iron images by some god or devil, how can they come to life?'

'There is witchcraft in the moon,' she shuddered. '*He* pointed at the moon; while the moon shines on them, they live. So I believe.'

'But we were not pursued,' muttered Conan, glancing toward the brooding ruins. 'You might have dreamed they moved. I am of a mind to return and see.'

'No, no!' she cried, clutching him desperately. 'Perhaps the spell upon them holds them in the hall. Do not go back! They will rend you limb from limb! Oh, Conan, let us go into our boat and flee this awful island! Surely the Hyrkanian ship has passed us now! Let us go!'

So frantic was her pleading that Conan was impressed. His curiosity in regard to the images was balanced by his superstition. Foes of flesh and blood he did not fear, however great the odds, but any hint of the supernatural roused all the dim monstrous instincts of fear that are the heritage of the barbarian.

He took the girl's hand and they went down the slope and plunged into the dense woods, where the leaves whispered, and nameless night-birds murmured drowsily. Under the trees the shadows clustered thick, and Conan swerved to avoid the denser patches. His eyes roved continuously from side to side, and often flitted into the branches above them. He went quickly yet warily, his arm girdling the girl's waist so strongly that she felt as if she were being carried rather than guided. Neither spoke. The only sound was the girl's quick nervous panting, the rustle of her small feet in the grass. So they came through the trees to the edge of the water, shimmering like molten silver in the moonlight.

'We should have brought fruit for food,' muttered Conan; 'but doubtless we'll find other islands. As well leave now as later; it's but a few hours till dawn—'

His voice trailed away. The painter was still made fast to the looping root. But at the other end was only a smashed and shattered ruin, half submerged in the shallow water.

A stifled cry escaped Olivia. Conan wheeled and faced the dense shadows, a crouching image of menace. The noise of the night-birds was suddenly silent. A brooding stillness reigned over the woods. No breeze moved the branches, yet somewhere the leaves stirred faintly.

Quick as a great cat Conan caught up Olivia and ran. Through the shadows he raced like a phantom, while somewhere above and behind them sounded a curious rushing among the leaves, that implacably drew closer and closer. Then the moonlight burst full upon their faces, and they were speeding up the slope of the plateau.

At the crest Conan laid Olivia down, and turned to glare back at the gulf of shadows they had just quitted. The leaves shook in a sudden breeze; that was all. He shook his mane with an angry growl. Olivia crept to his feet like a frightened child. Her eyes looked up at him, dark wells of horror.

'What are we to do, Conan?' she whispered.

He looked at the ruins, stared again into the woods below.

'We'll go to the cliffs,' he declared, lifting her to her feet. 'Tomorrow I'll make a raft, and we'll trust our luck to the sea again.'

'It was not—not *they* that destroyed our boat?' It was half question, half assertion.

He shook his head, grimly taciturn.

Every step of the way across that moon-haunted plateau was a sweating terror for Olivia, but no black shapes stole subtly from the looming ruins, and at last they reached the foot of the crags, which rose stark and gloomily majestic above them. There Conan halted in some uncertainty, at last selecting a place sheltered by a broad ledge, nowhere near any trees.

'Lie down and sleep if you can, Olivia,' he said. 'I'll keep watch.'

But no sleep came to Olivia, and she lay watching the distant ruins and the wooded rim until the stars paled, the east whitened, and dawn in rose and gold struck fire from the dew on the grass-blades.

She rose stiffly, her mind reverting to all the happenings of the night. In the morning light some of its terrors seemed like figments of an overwrought imagination. Conan strode over to her, and his words electrified her.

'Just before dawn I heard the creak of timbers and the rasp and clack of cordage and oars. A ship has put in and anchored at the beach not far away—probably the ship whose sail we saw yesterday. We'll go up the cliffs and spy on her.'

Up they went, and lying on their bellies among the boulders, saw a painted mast jutting up beyond the trees to the west.

'An Hyrkanian craft, from the cut of her rigging,' muttered Conan. 'I wonder if the crew—'

A distant medley of voices reached their ears, and creeping to the southern edge of the cliffs, they saw a motley horde emerge from the fringe of trees along the western rim of the plateau, and stand there a space in debate. There was much flourishing of arms, brandishing of swords, and loud rough argument. Then the whole band started across the plateau toward the ruins, at a slant that would take them close by the foot of the cliffs.

'Pirates!' whispered Conan, a grim smile on his thin lips. 'It's an Hyrkanian galley they've captured. Here—crawl among these rocks.

'Don't show yourself unless I call to you,' he instructed, having secreted her to his satisfaction among a tangle of boulders along the crest of the cliffs. 'I'm going to meet these dogs. If I succeed in my plan, all will be well, and we'll sail away with them. If I don't succeed—well, hide yourself in the rocks until they're gone, for no devils on this island are as cruel as these sea-wolves.'

And tearing himself from her reluctant grasp, he swung quickly down the cliffs.

Looking fearfully from her eyrie, Olivia saw the band had neared the foot of the cliffs. Even as she looked, Conan stepped out from among the boulders and faced them, sword in hand. They gave back with yells of menace and surprize; then halted uncertainly to glare at this figure which had appeared so suddenly from the rocks. There were some seventy of them, a wild horde made up of men from many nations: Kothians, Zamorians, Brythunians, Corinthians, Shemites. Their features reflected the wildness of their natures. Many bore the scars of the lash or the branding-iron. There were cropped ears, slit noses, gaping eye-sockets, stumps of wrists—marks of the hangman as well as scars of battle. Most of them were half naked, but the garments they wore were fine; gold-braided jackets, satin girdles, silken breeches, tattered, stained with tar and blood, vied with pieces of silver-chased armor. Jewels glittered in nose-rings and ear-rings, and in the hilts of their daggers.

Over against this bizarre mob stood the tall Cimmerian in strong contrast with his hard bronzed limbs and clean-cut vital features.

'Who are you?' they roared.

'Conan the Cimmerian!' His voice was like the deep challenge of a lion. 'One of the Free Companions. I mean to try my luck with the Red Brotherhood. Who's your chief?'

'I, by Ishtar!' bellowed a bull-like voice, as a huge figure swaggered forward: a giant, naked to the waist, where his capacious belly was girdled by a wide sash that upheld voluminous silken pantaloons. His head was shaven except for a scalp-lock, his mustaches dropped over a rat-trap mouth. Green Shemitish slippers with upturned toes were on his feet, a long straight sword in his hand.

Conan stared and glared.

'Sergius of Khrosha, by Crom!'

'Aye, by Ishtar!' boomed the giant, his small black eyes glittering with hate. 'Did you think I had forgot? Ha! Sergius never forgets an enemy. Now I'll hang you up by the heels and skin you alive. At him, lads!'

'Aye, send your dogs at me, big-belly,' sneered Conan with bitter scorn. 'You were always a coward, you Kothic cur.'

'Coward! To me?' The broad face turned black with passion. 'On guard, you northern dog! I'll cut out your heart!'

In an instant the pirates had formed a circle about the rivals, their eyes blazing, their breath sucking between their teeth in bloodthirsty enjoyment. High up among the crags Olivia watched, sinking her nails into her palms in her painful excitement.

Without formality the combatants engaged, Sergius coming in with a rush, quick on his feet as a giant cat, for all his bulk. Curses hissed between his clenched teeth as he lustily swung and parried. Conan fought in silence, his eyes slits of blue bale-fire.

The Kothian ceased his oaths to save his breath. The only sounds were the quick scuff of feet on the sward, the panting of the pirate, the ring and clash of steel. The swords flashed like white fire in the early sun, wheeling and circling. They seemed to recoil from each other's contact, then leap together again instantly. Sergius was giving back; only his superlative skill had saved him thus far from the blinding speed of the Cimmerian's onslaught. A louder clash of steel, a sliding rasp, a choking cry—from the pirate horde a fierce yell split the morning as Conan's sword plunged through their captain's massive body. The point quivered an instant from between Sergius's shoulders, a hand's breadth of white fire in the sunlight; then the Cimmerian wrenched back his steel and the pirate chief fell heavily, face down, and lay in a widening pool of blood, his broad hands twitching for an instant.

Conan wheeled toward the gaping corsairs.

'Well, you dogs!' he roared. 'I've sent your chief to hell. What says the law of the Red Brotherhood?'

Before any could answer, a rat-faced Brythunian, standing behind his fellows, whirled a sling swiftly and deadly. Straight as an arrow sped the stone to its mark, and Conan reeled and fell as a tall tree falls to the woodsman's ax. Up on the cliff Olivia caught at the boulders for support. The scene swam dizzily before her eyes; all she could see was the Cimmerian lying limply on the sward, blood oozing from his head.

The rat-faced one yelped in triumph and ran to stab the prostrate man, but a lean Corinthian thrust him back.

'What, Aratus, would you break the law of the Brotherhood, you dog?'

'No law is broken,' snarled the Brythunian.

'No law? Why, you dog, this man you have just struck down is by just rights our captain!'

'Nay!' shouted Aratus. 'He was not of our band, but an outsider. He had not been admitted to fellowship. Slaying Sergius does not make him captain, as would have been the case had one of us killed him.'

'But he wished to join us,' retorted the Corinthian. 'He said so.'

At that a great clamor arose, some siding with Aratus, some with the Corinthian, whom they called Ivanos. Oaths flew thick, challenges were passed, hands fumbled at sword-hilts.

At last a Shemite spoke up above the clamor: 'Why do you argue over a dead man?'

'He's not dead,' answered the Corinthian, rising from beside the prostrate Cimmerian. 'It was a glancing blow; he's only stunned.'

At that the clamor rose anew, Aratus trying to get at the senseless man and Ivanos finally bestriding him, sword in hand, and defying all and sundry. Olivia sensed that it was not so much in defense of Conan that the Corinthian took his stand, but in opposition to Aratus. Evidently these men had been Sergius's lieutenants, and there was no love lost between them. After more arguments, it was decided to bind Conan and take him along with them, his fate to be voted on later.

The Cimmerian, who was beginning to regain consciousness, was bound with leather girdles, and then four pirates lifted him, and with many complaints and curses, carried him along with the band, which took up its journey across the plateau once more. The body of Sergius was left where it had fallen; a sprawling, unlovely shape on the sun-washed sward.

Up among the rocks, Olivia lay stunned by the disaster. She was incapable of speech or action, and could only lie there and stare with horrified eyes as the brutal horde dragged her protector away.

How long she lay there, she did not know. Across the plateau she saw the pirates reach the ruins and enter, dragging their captive. She saw them swarming in and out of the doors and crevices, prodding into the heaps of debris, and clambering about the walls. After awhile a score of them came back across the plateau and vanished among the trees on the western rim, dragging the body of Sergius after them, presumably to cast into the sea. About the ruins the others were cutting down trees and securing material for a fire. Olivia heard their shouts, unintelligible in the distance, and she heard the voices of those who had gone into the woods, echoing among the trees. Presently they came back into sight, bearing casks of liquor and leathern sacks of food. They headed for the ruins, cursing lustily under their burdens.

Of all this Olivia was but mechanically cognizant. Her overwrought brain was almost ready to collapse. Left alone and unprotected, she realized how much the protection of the Cimmerian had meant to her. There intruded vaguely a wonderment at the mad pranks of Fate, that could make the daughter of a king the companion of a red-handed barbarian. With it came a revulsion toward her own kind. Her father, and Shah Amurath, they were civilized men. And from them she had had only suffering. She had never encountered any civilized man who treated her with kindness unless there was an ulterior motive behind his actions. Conan had shielded her, protected her, and—so far—demanded nothing in return. Laying her head in her rounded arms she wept, until distant shouts of ribald revelry roused her to her own danger.

She glanced from the dark ruins about which the fantastic figures, small in the distance, weaved and staggered, to the dusky depths of the green forest. Even if her terrors in the ruins the night before had been only dreams, the menace that lurked in those green leafy depths below was no figment of nightmare. Were Conan slain or carried away captive, her only choice would lie between giving herself up to the human wolves of the sea, or remaining alone on that devil-haunted island.

As the full horror of her situation swept over her, she fell forward in a swoon.

3

The sun was hanging low when Olivia regained her senses. A faint wind wafted to her ears distant shouts and snatches of ribald song. Rising cautiously, she looked out across the plateau. She saw the pirates clustered about a great fire outside the ruins, and her heart leaped as a group emerged from the interior dragging some object she knew was Conan. They propped him against the wall, still evidently bound fast, and there ensued a long discussion, with much brandishing of weapons. At last they dragged him back into the hall, and took up anew the business of ale-guzzling. Olivia sighed; at least she knew that the Cimmerian still lived. Fresh determination steeled her. As soon as night fell, she would steal to those grim ruins and free him or be taken herself in the attempt. And she knew it was not selfish interest alone which prompted her decision.

With this in mind she ventured to creep from her refuge to pluck and eat nuts which grew sparsely near at hand. She had not eaten since the day before. It was while so occupied that she was troubled by a sensation of being watched. She scanned the rocks nervously, then, with a shuddering suspicion, crept to the north edge of the cliff and gazed down into the waving green mass below, already dusky with the sunset. She saw nothing; it was impossible that she could be seen, when not on the cliff's edge, by anything lurking in those woods. Yet she distinctly felt the glare of hidden eyes, and felt that *something* animate and sentient was aware of her presence and her hiding-place.

Stealing back to her rocky eyrie, she lay watching the distant ruins until the dusk of night masked them, and she marked their position by the flickering flames about which black figures leaped and cavorted groggily.

Then she rose. It was time to make her attempt. But first she stole back to the northern edge of the cliffs, and looked down into the woods that bordered the beach. And as she strained her eyes in the dim starlight, she stiffened, and an icy hand touched her heart.

Far below her something moved. It was as if a black shadow detached itself from the gulf of shadows below her. It moved slowly up the sheer face of the cliff—a vague bulk, shapeless in the semi-darkness. Panic caught Olivia by the throat, and she struggled with the scream that tugged at her lips. Turning, she fled down the southern slope.

That flight down the shadowed cliffs was a nightmare in which she slid and scrambled, catching at jagged rocks with cold fingers. As she tore her tender skin and bruised her soft limbs on the rugged boulders over which Conan had so lightly lifted her, she realized again her dependence on the iron-thewed barbarian. But this thought was but one in a fluttering maelstrom of dizzy fright.

The descent seemed endless, but at last her feet struck the grassy levels, and in a very frenzy of eagerness she sped away toward the fire that burned like the red heart of night. Behind her, as she fled, she heard a shower of stones rattle down the steep slope, and the sound lent wings to her heels. What grisly climber dislodged those stones she dared not try to think.

Strenuous physical action dissipated her blind terror somewhat and before she had reached the ruin, her mind was clear, her reasoning faculties alert, though her limbs trembled from her efforts.

She dropped to the sward and wriggled along on her belly until, from behind a small tree that had escaped the axes of the pirates, she watched her enemies. They had completed their supper, but were still drinking, dipping pewter mugs or jewelled goblets into the broken heads of the wine-casks. Some were already snoring drunkenly on the grass, while others had staggered into the ruins. Of Conan she saw nothing. She lay there, while the dew formed on the grass about her and the leaves overhead, and the men about the fire cursed, gambled and argued. There were only a few about the fire; most of them had gone into the ruins to sleep.

She lay watching them, her nerves taut with the strain of waiting, the flesh crawling between her shoulders at the thought of what might be watching her in turn—of what might be stealing up behind her. Time dragged on leaden feet. One by one the revellers sank down in drunken slumber, until all were stretched senseless beside the dying fire.

Olivia hesitated—then was galvanized by a distant glow rising through the trees. The moon was rising!

With a gasp she rose and hurried toward the ruins. Her flesh crawled as she tiptoed among the drunken shapes that sprawled beside the gaping portal. Inside were many more; they shifted and mumbled in their besotted dreams, but none awakened as she glided among them. A sob of joy rose to her lips as she saw Conan. The Cimmerian was wide awake, bound upright to a pillar, his eyes gleaming in the faint reflection of the waning fire outside.

Picking her way among the sleepers, she approached him. Lightly as she had come, he had heard her; had seen her when first framed in the portal. A faint grin touched his hard lips.

She reached him and clung to him an instant. He felt the quick beating of her heart against his breast. Through a broad crevice in the wall stole a beam of moonlight, and the air was instantly supercharged with subtle tension. Conan felt it and stiffened. Olivia felt it and gasped. The sleepers snored on. Bending quickly, she drew a dagger from its senseless owner's belt, and set to work on Conan's bonds. They were sail cords, thick and heavy, and tied with the craft of a sailor. She toiled desperately, while the tide of moonlight crept slowly across the floor toward the feet of the crouching black figures between the pillars.

Her breath came in gasps; Conan's wrists were free, but his elbows and legs were still bound fast. She glanced fleetingly at the figures along the walls—waiting, waiting. They seemed to watch her with the awful patience of the undead. The drunkards beneath her feet began to stir and groan in their sleep. The moonlight crept down the hall, touching the black feet. The cords fell from Conan's arms, and taking the dagger from her, he ripped the bonds from his legs with a single quick slash. He stepped out from the pillar, flexing his limbs, stoically enduring the agony of returning circulation. Olivia crouched against him, shaking like a leaf. Was it some trick of the moonlight that touched the eyes of the black figures with fire, so that they glimmered redly in the shadows?

Conan moved with the abruptness of a jungle cat. Catching up his sword from where it lay in a stack of weapons near by, he lifted Olivia lightly from her feet and glided through an opening that gaped in the ivy-grown wall.

No word passed between them. Lifting her in his arms he set off swiftly across the moon-bathed sward. Her arms about his iron neck, the Ophirean closed her eyes, cradling her dark curly head against his massive shoulder. A delicious sense of security stole over her.

In spite of his burden, the Cimmerian crossed the plateau swiftly, and Olivia, opening her eyes, saw that they were passing under the shadow of the cliffs.

'Something climbed the cliffs,' she whispered. 'I heard it scrambling behind me as I came down.'

'We'll have to chance it,' he grunted.

'I am not afraid—now,' she sighed.

'You were not afraid when you came to free me, either,' he answered. 'Crom, what a day it has been! Such haggling and wrangling I never heard. I'm nearly deaf. Aratus wished to cut out my heart, and Ivanos refused, to spite Aratus, whom he hates. All day long they snarled and spat at one another, and the crew quickly grew too drunk to vote either way—'

He halted suddenly, an image of bronze in the moonlight. With a quick gesture he tossed the girl lightly to one side and behind him. Rising to her knees on the soft sward, she screamed at what she saw.

Out of the shadows of the cliffs moved a monstrous shambling bulk—an anthropomorphic horror, a grotesque travesty of creation.

In general outline it was not unlike a man. But its face, limned in the bright moonlight, was bestial, with close-set ears, flaring nostrils, and a great flabby-lipped mouth in which gleamed white tusk-like fangs. It was covered with shaggy grayish hair, shot with silver which shone in the moonlight, and its great misshapen paws hung nearly to the earth. Its bulk was tremendous; as it stood on its short bowed legs, its bullet-head rose above that of the man who faced it; the sweep of the hairy breast and giant shoulders was breathtaking; the huge arms were like knotted trees.

The moonlight scene swam, to Olivia's sight. This, then, was the end of the trail—for what human being could withstand the fury of that hairy mountain of thews and ferocity? Yet as she stared in wide-eyed horror at the bronzed figure facing the monster, she sensed a kinship in the antagonists that was almost appalling. This was less a struggle between man and beast than a conflict between two creatures of the wild, equally merciless and ferocious. With a flash of white tusks, the monster charged.

The mighty arms spread wide as the beast plunged, stupefyingly quick for all his vast bulk and stunted legs.

Conan's action was a blur of speed Olivia's eye could not follow. She only saw that he evaded that deadly grasp, and his sword, flashing like a jet of white lightning, sheared through one of those massive arms between shoulder and elbow. A great spout of blood deluged the sward as the severed member fell, twitching horribly, but even as the sword bit through, the other malformed hand locked in Conan's black mane.

Only the iron neck-muscles of the Cimmerian saved him from a broken neck that instant. His left hand darted out to clamp on the beast's squat throat, his left knee was jammed hard against the brute's hairy belly. Then began a terrific struggle, which lasted only seconds, but which seemed like ages to the paralyzed girl.

The ape maintained his grasp in Conan's hair, dragging him toward the tusks that glistened in the moonlight. The Cimmerian resisted this effort, with his left arm rigid as iron, while the sword in his right hand, wielded like a butcher-knife, sank again and again into the groin, breast and belly of his captor. The beast took its punishment in awful silence, apparently unweakened by the blood that gushed from its ghastly wounds. Swiftly the terrible strength of the anthropoid overcame the leverage of braced arm and knee. Inexorably Conan's arm bent under the strain; nearer and nearer he was drawn to the slavering jaws that gaped for his life. Now the blazing eyes of the barbarian glared into the bloodshot eyes of the ape. But as Conan tugged vainly at his sword, wedged deep in the hairy body, the frothing jaws snapped spasmodically shut, an inch from the Cimmerian's face, and he was hurled to the sward by the dying convulsions of the monster.

Olivia, half fainting, saw the ape heaving, thrashing and writhing, gripping, man-like, the hilt that jutted from its body. A sickening instant of this, then the great bulk quivered and lay still.

Conan rose and limped over to the corpse. The Cimmerian breathed heavily, and walked like a man whose joints and muscles have been wrenched and twisted almost to their limit of endurance. He felt his bloody scalp and swore at the sight of the long black red-stained strands still grasped in the monster's shaggy hand.

'Crom!' he panted. 'I feel as if I'd been racked! I'd rather fight a dozen men. Another instant and he'd have bitten off my head. Blast him, he's torn a handful of my hair out by the roots.'

Gripping his hilt with both hands he tugged and worked it free. Olivia stole close to clasp his arm and stare down wide-eyed at the sprawling monster.

'What—what is it?' she whispered.

'A gray man-ape,' he grunted. 'Dumb, and man-eating. They dwell in the hills that border the eastern shore of this sea. How this one got to this island, I can't say. Maybe he floated here on driftwood, blown out from the mainland in a storm.'

'And it was he that threw the stone?'

'Yes; I suspected what it was when we stood in the thicket and I saw the boughs bending over our heads. These creatures always lurk in the deepest woods they can find, and seldom emerge. What brought him into the open, I can't say, but it was lucky for us; I'd have had no chance with him among the trees.'

'It followed me,' she shivered. 'I saw it climbing the cliffs.'

'And following his instinct, he lurked in the shadow of the cliff, instead of following you out across the plateau. His kind are creatures of darkness and the silent places, haters of sun and moon.'

'Do you suppose there are others?'

'No, else the pirates had been attacked when they went through the woods. The gray ape is wary, for all his strength, as shown by his hesitancy in falling upon us in the thicket. His lust for you must have been great, to have driven him to attack us finally in the open. What—'

He started and wheeled back toward the way they had come. The night had been split by an awful scream. It came from the ruins.

Instantly there followed a mad medley of yells, shrieks and cries of blasphemous agony. Though accompanied by a ringing of steel, the sounds were of massacre rather than battle.

Conan stood frozen, the girl clinging to him in a frenzy of terror. The clamor rose to a crescendo of madness, and then the Cimmerian turned and went swiftly toward the rim of the plateau, with its fringe of moon-limned trees. Olivia's legs were trembling so that she could not walk; so he carried her, and her heart calmed its frantic pounding as she nestled into his cradling arms.

They passed under the shadowy forest, but the clusters of blackness held no terrors, the rifts of silver discovered no grisly shape. Night-birds murmured slumberously. The yells of slaughter dwindled behind them, masked in the distance to a confused jumble of sound. Somewhere a parrot called, like an eery echo: '*Yagkoolan yok tha, xuthalla!*' So they came to the tree-fringed water's edge and saw the galley lying at anchor, her sail shining white in the moonlight. Already the stars were paling for dawn.

4

In the ghastly whiteness of dawn a handful of tattered, blood-stained figures staggered through the trees and out on to the narrow beach. There were forty-four of them, and they were a cowed and demoralized band. With panting haste they plunged into the water and began to wade toward the galley, when a stern challenge brought them up standing.

Etched against the whitening sky they saw Conan the Cimmerian standing in the bows, sword in hand, his black mane tossing in the dawn wind.

'Stand!' he ordered. 'Come no nearer. What would you have, dogs?'

'Let us come aboard!' croaked a hairy rogue fingering a bloody stump of ear. 'We'd be gone from this devil's island.'

'The first man who tries to climb over the side, I'll split his skull,' promised Conan.

They were forty-four to one, but he held the whip-hand. The fight had been hammered out of them.

'Let us come aboard, good Conan,' whined a red-sashed Zamorian, glancing fearfully over his shoulder at the silent woods. 'We have been so mauled, bitten, scratched and rended, and are so weary from fighting and running, that not one of us can lift a sword.'

'Where is that dog Aratus?' demanded Conan.

'Dead, with the others! It was devils fell upon us! They were rending us to pieces before we could awake—a dozen good rovers died in their sleep. The ruins were full of flame-eyed shadows, with tearing fangs and sharp talons.'

'Aye!' put in another corsair. 'They were the demons of the isle, which took the forms of molten images, to befool us. Ishtar! We lay down to sleep among them. We are no cowards. We fought them as long as mortal man may strive against the powers of darkness. Then we broke away and left them tearing at the corpses like jackals. But surely they'll pursue us.'

'Aye, let us come aboard!' clamored a lean Shemite. 'Let us come in peace, or we must come sword in hand, and though we be so weary you will doubtless slay many of us, yet you can not prevail against us many.'

'Then I'll knock a hole in the planks and sink her,' answered Conan grimly. A frantic chorus of expostulation rose, which Conan silenced with a lion-like roar.

'Dogs! Must I aid my enemies? Shall I let you come aboard and cut out my heart?'

'Nay, nay!' they cried eagerly. 'Friends—friends, Conan. We are thy comrades! We be all lusty rogues together. We hate the king of Turan, not each other.'

Their gaze hung on his brown, frowning face.

'Then if I am one of the Brotherhood,' he grunted, 'the laws of the Trade apply to me; and since I killed your chief in fair fight, then I am your captain!'

There was no dissent. The pirates were too cowed and battered to have any thought except a desire to get away from that island of fear. Conan's gaze sought out the blood-stained figure of the Corinthian.

'How, Ivanos!' he challenged. 'You took my part, once. Will you uphold my claims again?'

'Aye, by Mitra!' The pirate, sensing the trend of feeling, was eager to ingratiate himself with the Cimmerian. 'He is right, lads; he is our lawful captain!'

A medley of acquiescence rose, lacking enthusiasm perhaps, but with sincerity accentuated by the feel of the silent woods behind them which might mask creeping ebony devils with red eyes and dripping talons.

'Swear by the hilt,' Conan demanded.

Forty-four sword-hilts were lifted toward him, and forty-four voices blended in the corsair's oath of allegiance.

Conan grinned and sheathed his sword. 'Come aboard, my bold swashbucklers, and take the oars.'

He turned and lifted Olivia to her feet, from where she had crouched shielded by the gunwales.

'And what of me, sir?' she asked.

'What would you?' he countered, watching her narrowly.

'To go with you, wherever your path may lie!' she cried, throwing her white arms about his bronzed neck.

The pirates, clambering over the rail, gasped in amazement.

'To sail a road of blood and slaughter?' he questioned. 'This keel will stain the blue waves crimson wherever it plows.'

'Aye, to sail with you on blue seas or red,' she answered passionately. 'You are a barbarian, and I am an outcast, denied by my people. We are both pariahs, wanderers of earth. Oh, take me with you!'

With a gusty laugh he lifted her to his fierce lips.

'I'll make you Queen of the Blue Sea! Cast off there, dogs! We'll scorch King Yildiz's pantaloons yet, by Crom!'

www.ingramcontent.com/pod-product-compliance
Lightning Source LLC
La Vergne TN
LVHW100406181026
850499LV00037B/627